SNOW WHITE
AND THE
SEVEN DWARFS

For Grace Armstrong — J.A.
For Saskia, with love — B.D.

DK

LONDON, NEW YORK, MUNICH,
MELBOURNE, AND DELHI

First American Edition, 2002

2 03 04 05 10 9 8 7 6 5 4 3 2

Published in the United States by
DK Publishing, Inc.
375 Hudson Street
New York, NY 10014

DK Publishing offers special discounts for bulk purchases for sales promotions or premiums.
Specific, large-quantity needs can be met with special editions, including
personalized covers, excerpts of existing guides, and corporate imprints.
For more information, contact Special Markets Department, DK Publishing Inc.,
375 Hudson Street, New York, NY 10014 Fax: 800-600-9098.

Library of Congress Cataloging-in-Publication Data

Aiken, Joan, 1924-
    Snow White and the seven dwarfs / adapted by Joan Aiken ; illustrated by Belinda Downes.
        p. cm.
    Summary: Retells the story of a princess who escapes her wicked stepmother by hiding
out in the home of seven hospitable dwarfs.
    ISBN 0-7894-8799-3
    [1. Fairy tales. 2. Folklore–Germany.] I. Downes, Belinda, ill. II. Title.

PZ8.A266 Sn 2002
398.2'0943'02–dc21

2002067440

Color reproduction by Dot Gradations, UK
Printed and bound in Spain by Artes Graficas Toledo

see our complete
product line at
www.dk.com

SNOW WHITE
AND THE
SEVEN DWARFS

adapted by Joan Aiken
illustrated by Belinda Downes

DK Publishing, Inc.

A QUEEN sat sewing by the window on a winter day. The snow fell outside, the black boughs of the trees shook and trembled in the gale. A gust rattled the window pane and the queen pricked her finger with the needle.

"Oh!" she cried, as three drops of blood fell on her handkerchief. But then she smiled.

"I wish," she said, "that my little daughter, soon to be born, will have hair as black as winter bark, skin as white as that snow, and lips as red as those drops of blood. I wish that she may be as beautiful as this day."

And she wound the handkerchief around her finger and went on embroidering a hood for the baby, soon to be born.

Sure enough, when the little princess came into the world, no one had ever seen such a beautiful child. Her eyes were deep blue, her hair was as soft and black as the branches of trees in winter, her lips were as red as blood, and her skin as white as snow. So she was called Snow White.

She was friendly and kind to everybody, and the whole world loved her. Except for one person.

Sadly, her mother, the queen, had died when Snow White was born, and after a year of mourning, the king had married again. His choice was a bad one. The new queen, though very beautiful, was a witch, descended from a long line of witches. She had an evil nature, and she took a dislike to little Snow White from the very start. This dislike turned to hate as the child grew, for the queen could not bear the idea that anybody might be more beautiful than she was. And soon it became clear that Snow White's looks might surpass her own.

The queen had a magic mirror. It had been stolen, over a hundred years ago, by her great-great-grandmother from a powerful enchanter who lived far away in the eastern desert. The mirror was a round one, made of crystal and ivory, framed in a circle of rubies. It had the power of giving a true answer to any person who looked into its depths and asked it a question.

So, from time to time when she combed her hair and put on her crown the queen would take the mirror from its box, made of pear wood and lined with white doves' feathers, hold it in her hand, stare into its depths, and ask:

Mirror, mirror, in my hand,
Who is the fairest in the land?

Then a mist would cloud over the crystal surface of the mirror, and it would wait a moment in a sulky silence (for in truth the mirror disliked the queen and longed to return to its true owner). But it was obliged to tell the truth, always, and it would answer:

Not a soul in this land is seen
Half so handsome as you, O Queen!

But one day, when the princess Snow White was seven and the queen asked her question, the mirror replied in a tone of triumph:

Everyone's beauty must pass away,
You were the fairest till yesterday.
But now Snow White, the lovely maid,
Puts you completely in the shade.
Your time's over, better face it,
When youth is gone, you just can't chase it!

The queen was so enraged by this that she asked the same question again twice. She could not believe what she heard. Each time the mirror gave her the same reply. She slammed the glass back into its box and decided that Snow White must die, at once, without delay.

Luckily for her, the king was away on a long journey to the other side of his realm. The queen sent for her chief huntsman and told him to take Snow White far into the forest, kill her, and bury her.

The huntsman trembled with horror, but he did not dare disobey.

He told Snow White that he was going to take her on a picnic and they rode off into the forest, she on her pony, he on his big, trusty horse. But when they had gone a long, long way, his heart betrayed him. He took pity on the beautiful child. He could not bear to do what the wicked queen had ordered.

"You must run away," he told Snow White. "Run far into the forest and never come back, for your stepmother wants you dead."

"But I'm afraid! I'm afraid of the forest beasts!"

"They are not so dangerous as the queen!"

The huntsman left Snow White crying and trembling under a tree. He rode back to the palace, leading the pony, and told the queen that Snow White was dead.

Meanwhile, Snow White herself had wandered farther and farther into the forest, over seven hills and through seven valleys, until night was near and she was so tired that she could hardly drag herself along. She was terrified of the beasts she saw: bears and wolves, lynxes and savage wild boars — but they did not harm her.

Luckily, just after nightfall, she came in sight
of a little thatched cottage in a tidy clearing, with rows
of vegetables, a well, and a rose bush by the door covered with
roses. Snow White was also afraid of outlaws, and giants,
and dragons, and goblins, all of whom were said to live in the
forest, but this looked like such a neat, friendly dwelling that
she felt sure no wicked person lived there, so she tapped on
the door.

Nobody answered.

Well, I will just go in and sit down for a little
while, thought Snow White, whose legs were so
tired they would hardly hold her up.

So she opened the door and went in.

The cottage was as neat inside as the garden outside.

There was a table laid with a white cloth. On the cloth were seven little plates, seven little bowls, seven little knives, seven little spoons. There were seven little glasses, seven little loaves of bread. There was a bowl of fruits and nuts, a pitcher of milk, a platter of cheese. Over the fire hung a pot of warm soup, slowly cooking. Against the far wall there were seven little beds, covered with seven little patchwork quilts.

Snow White sat down on a stool to wait for the seven little people who lived there to come back.

But she was so hungry and thirsty that, after a while, she thought:

Well, I will just take a nibble from one loaf. They won't mind that, will they?

And then she thought:

Well, I will just take a sip of soup from one bowl. No one could object to that?

And then she thought:

Well, I will take a tiny drink of milk from one glass. They will hardly notice.

And then she thought:

Well, I will just take one apple from a bowl. There are nine, for I counted.

And then she thought:

Well, I will just take a small slice of cheese. It's a big piece of cheese. One slice won't show.

And then she thought:

Well, I will just take one grape from the bunch. One is neither here nor there.

And then she thought:

Well, I will just take one walnut. There's a whole bowlful after all.

Then, as the owners of the cottage still had not come home, and Snow White was so very, very tired and sad, she thought:

I will just lie down on one of these beds for a few minutes. They do look so comfortable.

So she did, and soon fell fast asleep.

Now, late in the evening, the owners of the house came home. They were seven dwarfs, brothers, who earned their living by mining gold and other precious metals in the mountains. They worked very hard every day from dawn till dusk.

As soon as they came in they took their places at the table to eat their supper.

Their names were Fred and Ted, Ike and Mike, Tim and Sim, and the youngest Sacheverell, who was called Sachie by all his brothers.

Sachie went to the fire to get the cauldron of soup. But Mike said: "Someone has chewed a bit off my bread!"

Ike said: "Someone has eaten soup from my bowl!"

Fred said: "Somebody has taken a drink from my glass!"

Ted said: "There's an apple core on my plate!"

Tim said: "Somebody has been eating the cheese!"

Sim said: "There's a grape missing!"

Sachie said: "There's a walnut shell on the table!"

All the dwarfs began to look around the room.

But Sachie found Snow White and whispered: "Shush! Hush, everybody! There's a most beautiful girl lying fast asleep on my bed!"

They all crowded around his bed and looked and wondered. And they all agreed, in whispers, that Snow White was the most beautiful girl they had ever seen.

"Don't wake her!" whispered Mike. "She does look so tired."

So they let her sleep in peace and Sachie, whose bed she lay in, slept on the floor.

In the morning, when Snow White awoke, they gave her a delicious breakfast of bread and milk and grapes. They were so kind and friendly that she felt able to trust them, so she told them that she was the king's daughter and that her wicked stepmother wanted to kill her.

"You must stay here with us," said Sachie at once. "Here in the forest you will be safe from her wickedness."

For, of course, he did not know about the queen's magic mirror.

"Yes, yes!" cried Fred and Ted, Ike and Mike, Sim and Tim. "Stay here with us and you shall be our dear little sister."

"But how can I repay you?" said Snow White anxiously, who wanted more than anything to stay.

"Very easily! You can sweep and dust for us, sew and mend for us, knit and cook for us."

Snow White had never done housework before but was happy to learn. She learned to care for the hens and geese, collect the eggs, pick peas and strawberries in the neat little garden, bake bread, and make butter and cheese. She was as happy as the day is long, far happier than she had ever been in the palace, with the queen's angry eyes always watching her, and the queen's harsh voice always scolding.

Weeks, and then months, went by. And then years went by.
But what of the queen? She had not looked in her mirror for a long time,
so confident was she that the huntsman had carried out her orders (for he,
prudent man, had left the palace after telling the lie about Snow White's
death). But one day, feeling low-spirited, for she had a pimple on her chin,
the queen decided to cheer herself up by having a talk with her mirror.
So she took it from its pear wood box and nest of doves' feathers:

> *Mirror, mirror, in my hand,*
> *Who is the fairest in the land?*

To her horrified surprise, the mirror replied, in tones of deep satisfaction:

> *Far in the forest, safe from spells,*
> *With seven brothers, Snow White dwells.*
> *In all the world there's none so fair,*
> *She is the best beyond compare.*
> *Little Snow White, the lovely maid,*
> *Puts you truly in the shade!*

The queen was so furious to hear that Snow White was
not dead that she nearly flung her mirror on the floor and
smashed it, but she restrained herself and slammed it back
into its box.

Then the queen put a smoke spell on the birds, to make
them tell her where in the forest Snow White lived.

The queen painted her face with walnut juice and disguised herself as an old peddler woman, before setting off for the dwarfs' cottage.

When she arrived there, she knocked at the door and called out: "Fine laces! Pretty ribbons! Buckles and buttons and beads! Braids and bangles and brooches! All cheap! All very, very cheap!"

Snow White had not seen any pretty things since she left the palace and by this time her own clothes were becoming worn and grimy. So she ran to open the door and let the pretend old woman in. And with the couple of pennies that were all she had in her pocket, she bought a pair of scarlet ribbons to fasten her bodice.

"Let me fasten them for you," said the queen, and she pulled the laces so tight that Snow White gasped and cried out and fell to the floor in a deep faint.

"That fixed you," said the queen, satisfied, and she darted off before the seven brothers returned.

When they came back, the dwarfs were horrified to see Snow White stretched out, apparently lifeless, on the ground.

Carefully, Sachie lifted her up, and then they could see that it was the tight ribbons that had done the mischief. When these were cut, Snow White began to breathe normally again, and soon she was as well as before. She told the story of what had happened, and the dwarfs had no trouble in guessing that it was the wicked queen who had come to the cottage. So they warned Snow White never again to let anybody into the house, and she promised that in the future she would be more careful.

Meanwhile, the wicked queen had hurried home to the palace, washed the walnut juice from her cheeks, and taken out her mirror:

Mirror, mirror, in my hand,
Who is the fairest in the land?

But to her rage and horror the mirror replied:

Far in the forest, safe from spells,
With seven brothers, Snow White dwells.
Snow White is fairest under the sun,
She makes you look like a cinnamon bun.

The queen was so furious that she almost threw her mirror out of the window. But she mastered her anger and slapped it back into its box. Then she disguised herself as a Spanish gypsy, and filled a tray with combs and spangled fans and hair ornaments of every kind, and made her way again over seven hills and seven valleys until she came to the dwarfs' cottage.

She banged on the door and called: "Fine combs to sell! Pearl and coral, ivory and tortoiseshell! Trinkets for your hair! Spangled and frosted and gilt! Come see! Come see!"

But Snow White put her head out of the window and said, "Lady, I am not allowed to let you in, or to leave the house. I cannot buy your wares."

And, however much the queen tried to persuade her, she would not open the door.

Then the queen said: "At least let me try this comb in your hair. See how well it would go with your bonny black locks!"

And she held up a comb that sparkled
with tiny stones bright as diamonds.
Snow White could not resist it and she put her
head farther out of the window and let the lady
set the comb in her hair.
But the comb was poisoned, and as soon as it touched
her head, Snow White fell backward onto the floor, stiff,
white, and cold, as if dead.
"That has surely done her in," gloated the queen, and
she hurried away, back to the palace.
She lost no time in getting out her mirror.

But meanwhile, the seven brothers had come home from their work in the mines, and were greatly shocked and distressed to find Snow White lying apparently dead on the floor. However, when they lifted her up, the poisoned comb fell from her hair, and she was soon well again. The brothers scolded her and warned her never again to be so foolish as to let any strange person into the house.

"But I didn't let her in!" pleaded Snow White.

"Well, don't buy anything from anybody," said Sachie.

And Snow White promised that she would not.

Far away, in the palace, the queen said to her mirror:

Mirror, mirror, in my hand,
Who is the fairest in the land?

And the mirror's answer came, loud and triumphant:

Far away, over seven hills,
With seven brothers, Snow White dwells.
She is the fairest under the moon,
She makes you look like a wrinkled prune!

The queen nearly burst with rage. And she very nearly threw her mirror into the fire, but stopped herself in time, and thrust it back into its box.

Then she used all her magic arts to make a poisoned apple. It looked exactly like a real juicy apple, bright red on one side, red and yellow striped on the other. It was so shiny and juicy and tempting that it would make anybody's mouth water just to look at it. One side was deadly, one side was harmless.

This time the queen disguised herself as a shepherdess with a flock of sheep and made her way back to the dwarfs' cottage.

She knocked on the door and called out: "Please, can you give me a drink of water? I am so very thirsty!"

Snow White put her head out of the window. "I am not allowed to let anybody in, but there is sweet water in the well. You are very welcome to wind yourself up a bucketful."

"Thank you, kind girl," said the pretend shepherdess. "Would you like a bite of my apple?" And she held the poisoned apple up to the window.

Snow White was very tempted. But she said, "No, I am not allowed."

"Oh, come," said the shepherdess. "This is a perfectly good apple. It won't hurt you. Look, I will take a bite of it myself." And she took a bite, careful to make sure that it was on the red and yellow striped side, which was harmless.

Snow White could not resist. She leaned out of the window and took a good big bite on the red side of the apple that the shepherdess held up to her.

As soon as the poisoned apple entered her mouth, she fell down dead, stiff and motionless on the cottage floor.

"Now she's really had it," said the queen, and she clapped her hands to make her magic flock of sheep disappear, and made her way back to the palace.

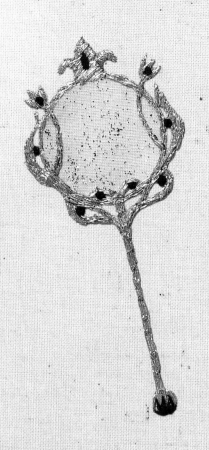

And this time, when
she asked the mirror:

Mirror, mirror, in my hand,
Who is the fairest in the land?

The mirror sighed, and replied:

You are the fairest, it must be said,
If poor Snow White is really dead.

For when the seven dwarfs came home that evening they could find
no way of reviving Snow White. They undid her ribbons, they combed
her hair, they washed her with water and wine. But she remained stiff
and cold and lifeless. The poor brothers were so sad that they
wept for a week.

"She was so kind and friendly," said Fred.

"And such a good cook," said Ted.

"And kept the house so tidy," said Mike.

"And told such lovely stories," said Ike.

"And mended our socks so well," said Tim.

"And sang such beautiful songs," said Sim.

"She was such a dear, good, sweet little
sister, and I loved her so," wailed Sachie.

As the brothers could not bear to part with Snow White, they made her a glass coffin and laid her in it, and set the coffin on the top of a great rock in the mountainside. And one of the brothers always kept watch beside it. All the birds came and grieved, too. An owl, a dove, and a hawk perched on the rock beside the coffin. The owl hooted, the dove cooed, and the hawk screamed. They did this day and night for a year, and then another year. And Snow White never changed; her lips remained as red as blood, her skin as white as snow, her hair soft and black as the winter bark of trees.

One day a young prince came riding by. He saw the coffin and he read the gold writing on it, which said: This is the body of Snow White, a king's daughter who was wickedly murdered.

The young prince was struck to the heart by the sight of Snow White. He fell in love with her on the spot. And he begged the dwarfs to let him take the glass coffin, with Snow White in it, back to his own castle in the mountains.

"I shall soon be King of the Western Isles," he told the dwarfs.

"I will take the best possible care of the beautiful lady; I promise you. Whereas if she stays here, you will all grow old in time, and who will keep watch over her then? Wild beasts may break the glass coffin."

At last the seven brothers agreed to let the prince take Snow White. He came back for her with a gold carriage drawn by six white horses and twenty knights in armor with black plumes on their helmets, to walk in front and behind.

But when the glass coffin was lifted off the rock, the movement shook the poisoned apple out of Snow White's mouth.

First she stirred, then she opened her eyes.

"Why, what has happened?" she said. "Where am I?"

Everybody was thunderstruck. The little dwarfs were delirious with joy. They danced, they shouted, they pulled the lid off the coffin, and Sachie helped Snow White to her feet. She stretched and trembled and laughed with happiness to be back among her friends again.

Then she saw the young prince kneeling at her feet.

"Beautiful Snow White, will you marry me?" he said. "And be Queen of the Western Isles? And make me the happiest of men?"

"Willingly, dear prince," said she, "if I may bring my friends the dwarfs with me."

And, of course, he said yes to that.

So the prince took Snow White back to his castle, and the invitations to a great wedding feast were sent out.

The wicked queen received an invitation and, anxious to make sure that her beauty was still unrivaled, she took her mirror out from its pear wood box and nest of doves' feathers:

Mirror, mirror, in my hand,
Who is the fairest in the land?

The mirror replied in a tone
of unmistakable glee:

Over the mountains, far away,
They celebrate Snow White's wedding day.
She will be Queen of the Western Isles,
And all her life will be crowned with smiles.
She is the fairest the whole world through,
She makes you look like a worn-out shoe!

When the wicked queen heard these
words she fell into such a passion
that she hurled the mirror onto
the marble floor and it
broke into a thousand
shimmering pieces.

42

One of these pierced the queen to the heart and she died on the spot.
The rest of the splinters flew together into a ruby and crystal cloud. The
wind carried this cloud far, far off to the desert where the enchanter lived
who had first made the mirror and was its true owner.

When the sparkling cloud came sailing down out of the sky, he caught
it in his hands and molded it into a ball. And he smiled as he did so.

"I will make sure that you are never stolen again," he said. "For you
have caused too much harm!"

The prince and Snow White had a splendid wedding feast. The seven dwarfs were there, gaily dressed in their best clothes. And the kind huntsman who had spared Snow White's life heard about it and came back from the foreign land where he had taken refuge. Best of all, Snow White's own father, who had long thought that his daughter was dead, came to give the bride away. And all the wedding guests feasted and danced and sang the whole night through.

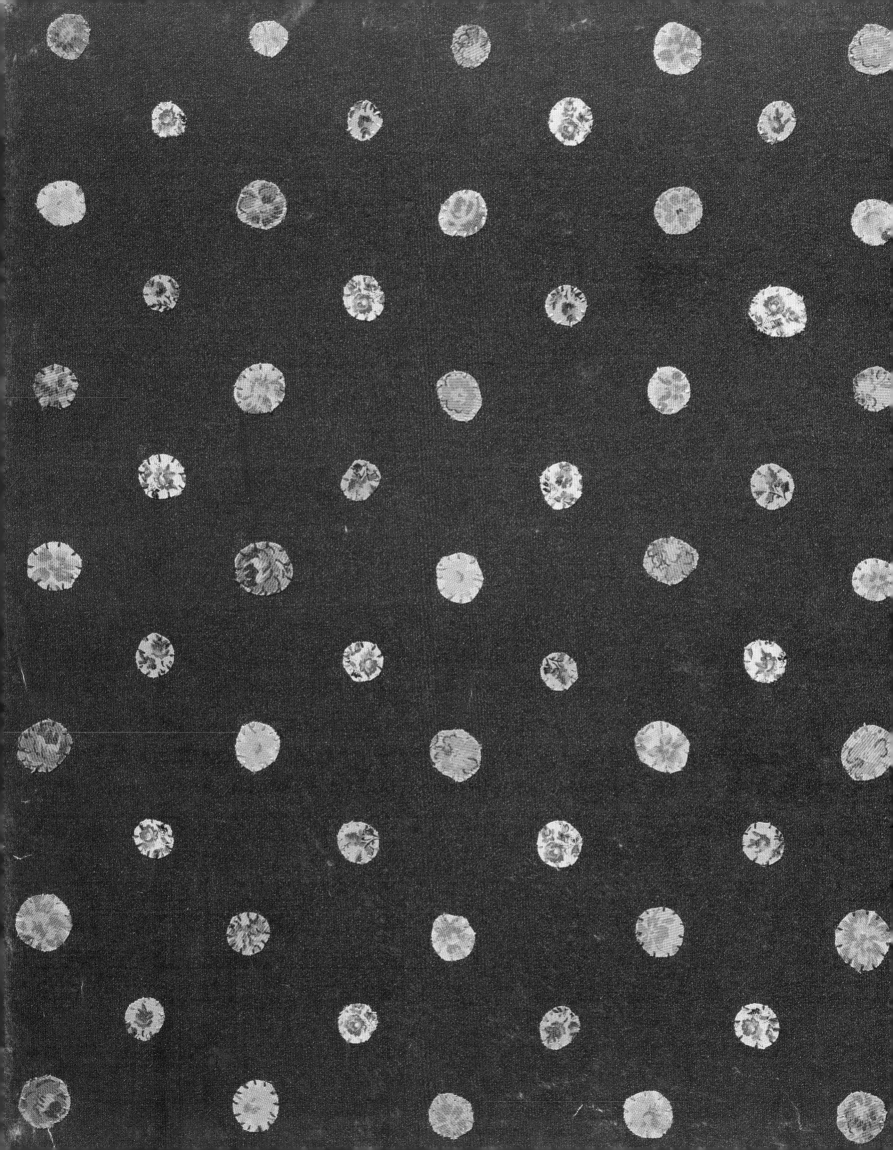

NOTE TO PARENTS

Perry's Not-So-Perfect Day
A story about good manners

Perry the Polite Porcupine always attempts to do and say the proper thing. His manners are impeccable, and he is always considerate of others. He tries his best to please his friends, but too often at his own expense. Then Perry finds out that you can say no and still be polite.

In addition to enjoying this story with your child, you can use it to teach a gentle lesson about the value of manners. Help your child understand that good manners make a good impression on others. Explain that when someone really doesn't want to do something, it's all right to say no, nicely but firmly.

You can also use this story to introduce the letter **P**. As you read about Perry the Polite Porcupine, ask your child to listen for all the words that start with **P,** and point to the objects that begin with **P**. When you've finished reading the story, your child will enjoy doing the activity at the end of the book.

Perry's Not-So-Perfect Day

Th⟨ … ⟩ Ruth Lerner Perle.
Ch⟨ … ⟩ rgo.
Co⟨ … ⟩
Lo⟨ … ⟩ ⟨ … ⟩.
Ed⟨ … ⟩